BOOK REVIEWS

Here's what people are saying:

A charming new book

from NEW YORK TIMES

It's a cozy book, and Fleishman's perky illustrations are right in keeping with the mood of snug familiarity.

from PUBLISHERS WEEKLY

WEEKLY READER CHILDREN'S BOOK CLUB PRESENTS

GUS LOVED HIS HAPPY HOME

JANE THAYER

Illustrated by Seymour Fleishman

·L·I·N·N·E·T · B·O·O·K·S·

Hamden, Connecticut

To Meg, Henry, Caroline, and Sam, with love.   J.T.

For Esther, Suzy, and Jenny.   S.F.

Weekly Reader Books offers several exciting
card and activity programs. For information,
write to WEEKLY READER BOOKS, P.O. Box 16636,
Columbus, Ohio 43216.

This book is a presentation of Weekly Reader Books.
Weekly Reader Books offers book clubs for children
from preschool through high school. For further
information write to: **Weekly Reader Books,** 4343
Equity Drive, Columbus, Ohio 43228.

Published by arrangement with Linnet Books, an
imprint of The Shoe String Press, Inc. Weekly
Reader is a federally registered trademark of Field
Publications.

Published 1989 as a Linnet Book,
an imprint of The Shoe String Press, Inc.,
Hamden, Connecticut 06514.
Manufactured in the United States.
Book design by Seymour Fleishman.

Library of Congress Cataloging-in-Publication Data
Thayer, Jane, 1904–
Gus loved his happy home / by Jane Thayer;
illustrated by Seymour Fleishman.
Summary: Gus the ghost neglects his housecleaning
chores while Mr. Frizzle is on vacation, and fears that
this dereliction of duty will cause him and his animal
friends to lose their home with Frizzle.
[1. Ghosts—Fiction.] I. Fleishman, Seymour, ill.
II. Title.
Pz7.W882Gt   1989   [E]—dc 19   88–36962
ISBN 0–208–02249–X

J   10   9   8   7   6   5   4   3   2   1

That old ghost called Gus
       loved his attic home
       in the Historical Museum.
He could bang
his bang-clank equipment.

He could hang up
the gorgeous sheets he wore.
His roommates were
Mouse the mouse
and a cat called Cora.
Cora was a very nice person.
She slept in the other twin bed.
Mouse preferred a sleeping bag.
He was a cranky old thing
but Gus said, "Mouse is Mouse."

Gus had this happy home
because he helped Mr. Frizzle,
who lived downstairs and ran the museum.
Mr. Frizzle was fussy about his museum,
and if anything went wrong
he lost his temper and shouted.
In fact, he always shouted at Gus
because he couldn't see a ghost
and never knew where he was.

But Gus got along
with Mr. Frizzle very well,
because he polished antique tables,
scrubbed away footprints
with his ghostly scrubbing brush,
and washed the windows twice a day.

Autumn came.
Mr. Frizzle put up a sign,

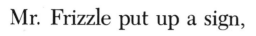

OPEN IN MAY

"I'm off to Florida," he yelled.
"Dust every day, Gus.
Don't open the door to strangers.
If everything's shipshape
when I get home,
you may keep your
attic apartment."

Gus dusted for a while.
Then he said, "I'll clean house
right before Frizzle gets home.
Now I'm going to have a little fun!"

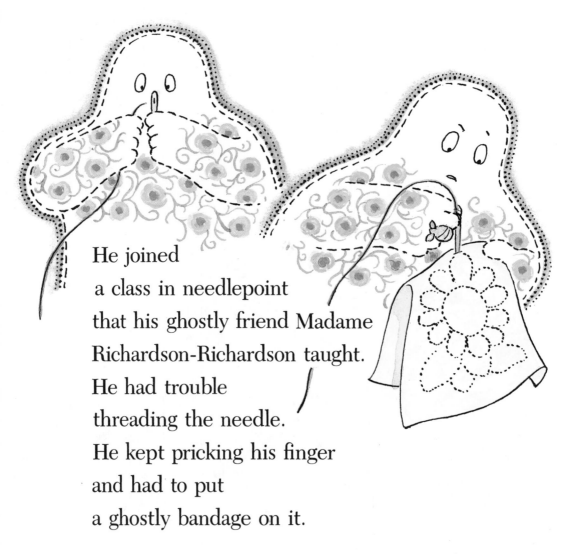

He joined
a class in needlepoint
that his ghostly friend Madame
Richardson-Richardson taught.
He had trouble
threading the needle.
He kept pricking his finger
and had to put
a ghostly bandage on it.

Madame said
maybe he'd prefer some sport.
"Good, I hate needlepoint!" said Gus.
Madame taught him to play croquet.
But she always won.
Then a ball whacked
into his ghostly toe.
Gus shouted,
"No more croquet!"
He went home mad
and bandaged his toe.

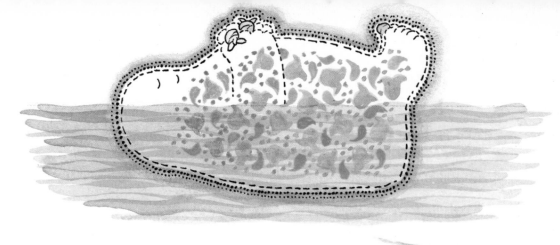

He tried swimming lessons.
He loved to float on his back.
He got a medal for swimming fast
and he learned some fancy dives.
"But what use is swimming
to a ghost, Cora?" he asked.
Cora said swimming was not her idea.
Snow came.
Gus took skiing lessons.
Down he tumbled
and sprained his ghostly ankle.

Cora said cooking was a cozy hobby.
He could start with fishcakes.
Mouse said he'd eat in
if Gus made cheesecake.
Cora and Mouse gained weight,
but Gus kept burning fingers
until every ghostly finger
wore a ghostly bandage.
"Enough fishcakes and cheesecakes!"
he yelled, and tore off his apron.
Mouse stalked out to eat
while Cora
looked reproachful.

Spring was in the air.
"Frizzle will be home soon.
I should do the spring cleaning,"
said Gus.
But he had spring fever
so he and Cora went looking
for violets.
They saw children flying kites.
"That looks like fun!"
cried Gus.

He asked Madame R–R
to make a flowered kite
to match his flowered sheet.

He took hold of the kite string.
Up went the kite.
Up went Gus, since he weighed
no more than a leaf.
"My goodness!" he gasped.
"See you later, Cora!"
"Have a nice day," Cora called.
Mouse muttered, "You're a fool."

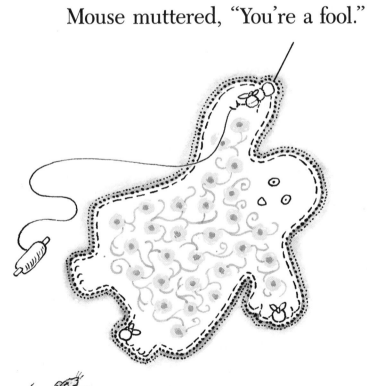

Up, up soared the kite
with Gus holding the string.
The museum grew smaller and smaller.
Cora and Mouse were specks.

The wind caught the kite
and Gus sailed off.
How fast he was going!
What fun!
Gus sailed joyfully on and on.

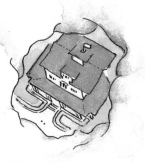

Then his bandaged hand began to hurt.
I can't hold on, he thought.
I've got to get home.
But the west wind was blowing him
further away.
Gus knew some useful ghostly words
and he ordered the wind to change.
He felt himself heading for home.
Through a hole in the clouds
he saw a tiny museum and two specks.
"I want to go down! Please!" he shouted.

But the roaring east wind
couldn't hear ghostly words.
Gus sailed off westward.
He was so upset
and his fingers were so tired
that without thinking he let go.
Off soared the flowered kite.
"I'll crash!
S.O.S.! Mayday! Help!" cried Gus.

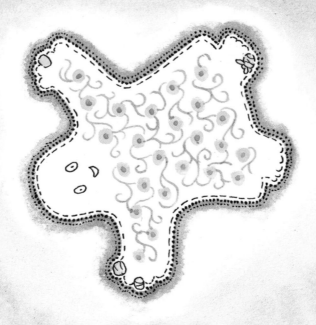

But he weighed no more than a leaf
so instead of crashing down to earth
he drifted in the air.
Gus was astonished.
He floated on his back.
He tried his best swimming stroke.
He was swimming in air.
Now he didn't want to go down.
"I'm flying! I'm flying!"
Gus shouted to the sky.

A flock of blackbirds came hurrying
home from the south.
Gus raced the birds
and got a feather for a prize.

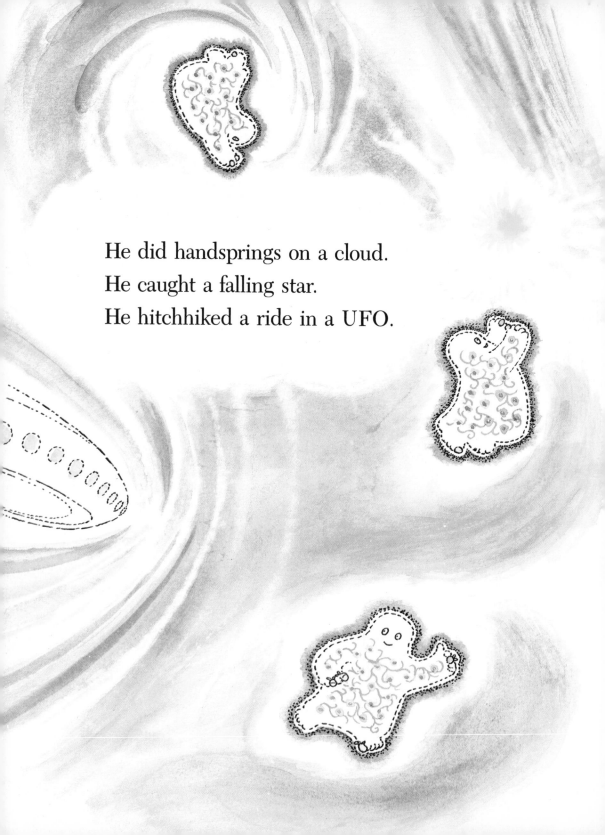

He did handsprings on a cloud.
He caught a falling star.
He hitchhiked a ride in a UFO.

Gus was having the time of his life
up there in the blue sky.
Suddenly he saw a jet plane
coming his way.

He did a jackknife dive
out of that huge jet's way.
That was the most fun!
But what did he see
as that jet thundered by?
He saw Mr. Frizzle.

Oh my goodness, Gus thought.
He's on his way home!
I haven't done
the spring cleaning
and I left the door unlocked.
He'll rent my apartment
to Madame R–R.
Oh, I'll have to stay up here
forever!
He thought of his happy home,
his bang-clank equipment,
Cora and cross old Mouse,
even Frizzle,
who wasn't such a bad fellow.
"No!" Gus shouted.
"I'm going to get there before he does!"

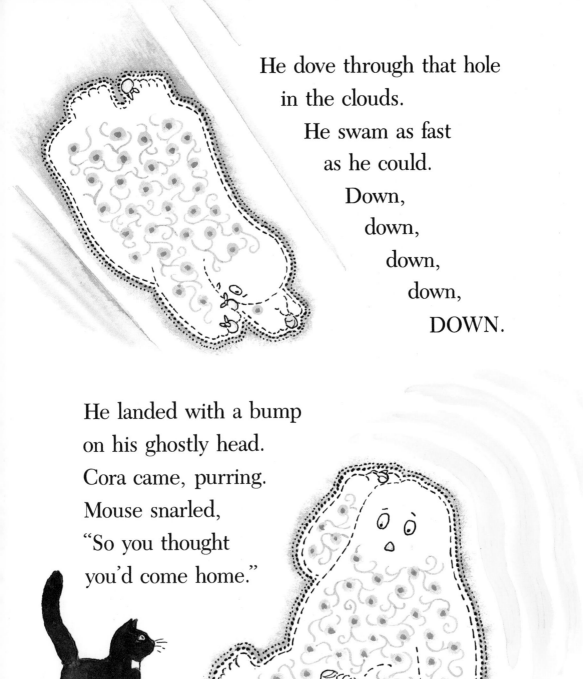

He dove through that hole
in the clouds.
He swam as fast
as he could.
Down,
down,
down,
down,
DOWN.

He landed with a bump
on his ghostly head.
Cora came, purring.
Mouse snarled,
"So you thought
you'd come home."

Gus rushed indoors.
He pulled out his ghostly
cleaning tools.

He swept,

dusted,

polished,

and mopped.

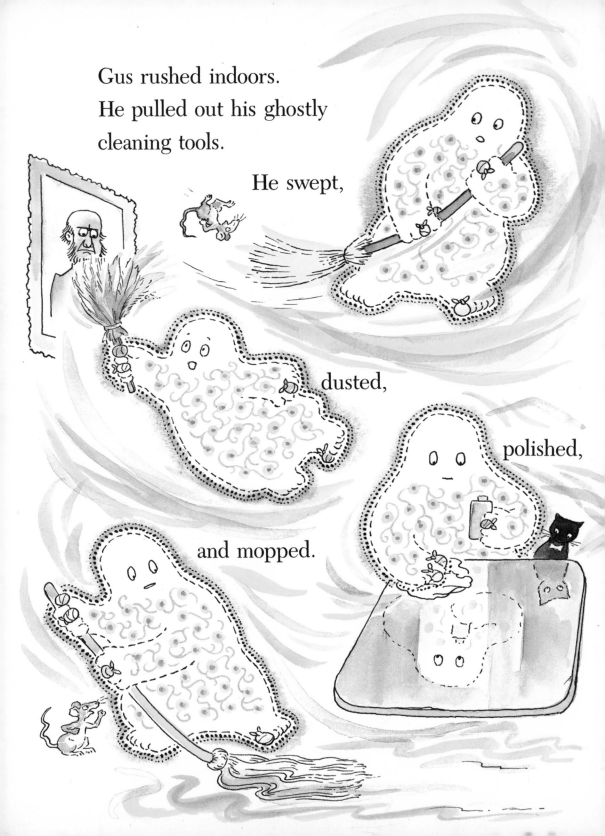

He finished the cleaning
as a taxi arrived
bringing Mr. Frizzle
from the airport.
Mr. Frizzle gazed
about the museum.
"All shipshape!"
he shouted.
Gus felt weak with relief.

He and Cora
climbed the stairs for a nap.
"It's a good thing
I had to let go
of that kite, Cora," Gus said.
"I could be miles away!
And isn't it lucky I could swim
and managed to get down!
But I had the most fun I've had
in my whole ghostly life!
I'm going flying
whenever Frizzle
gives me a day off.
Maybe I'll take you, Cora!"
Cora crawled under the bed.
"Oh well, stay home then," said Gus.

Suddenly he thought,
We almost lost our home.
Gently he patted his bed,
his bang-clank equipment,
the line for his flowered sheets.
He peeked in at Mouse,
snoring in his sleeping bag.
He was so happy
he wanted his friends
to be happy, too.

Gus went to the ghostly chest
where he kept supplies.
He took out some catnip.
"Come on out, Cora," he called.
He could see her handsome black whiskers
and topaz yellow eyes.
He took out some smelly cheese.
Mouse's nose twitched. His eyes popped open.
He tumbled out of his sleeping bag.
Gus tied their napkins cozily
under their chins, and he thought,
How I love, love, love my happy home.